Just One Of The Guys

"Hey, Caroline," Michael Hopkins called from the back of the classroom. "Can you help me?"

Caroline didn't see him, just two boys who were holding a huge piece of plywood. "Where are you, Michael?" she asked.

"Back here." He stuck his head around the edge of the wood. "This board is the bottom of our ring-toss booth. I'm marking where the pegs will go."

"What do I do?"

"Hammer a small nail through each mark in the front of the board," Michael said. "I'll watch from the back to make sure the nails come through in the right places." He pointed to a hammer and nails and disappeared behind the board again.

Caroline hit the first nail hard. She wondered if Michael would have asked her to help him if she'd been wearing a cute little pink dress. It wasn't that she wanted the guys to think she was helpless, but why couldn't they notice she was a *girl?*

Look for these books in the Caroline Zucker series:

Caroline Zucker
Gets Her Wish

by Jan Bradford
Illustrated by Marcy Ramsey

Troll Associates

Library of Congress Cataloging-in-Publication Data

Bradford, Jan.
   Caroline Zucker gets her wish / by Jan Bradford; illustrated by
Marcy Ramsey.
      p.   cm.
   Summary: Caroline makes exciting plans for her third grade class's
participation in the school fair and tries to convince her mother to
let her dress in a more attractive, feminine manner.
   ISBN 0-8167-2019-3 (lib. bdg.)   ISBN 0-8167-2020-7 (pbk.)
   [1. Schools—Fiction.   2. Self-perception—Fiction.]   I. Ramsey,
Marcy Dunn, ill.   II. Title.
PZ7.B7228Cas   1991
[Fic]-dc20   90-31549

A TROLL BOOK, published by Troll Associates
Mahwah, NJ 07430

10   9   8   7   6   5   4   3   2   1

1

GOOD NEWS!

Mrs. Nicks smiled at her third-grade class from behind her desk. "I have great news!"

Some of the kids groaned and Caroline Zucker knew exactly how they felt. You could never be sure what Mrs. Nicks would consider "great." Once she had gotten excited about a boring movie on plants. But another time, she had brought in a puppy for them to play with.

Caroline slid back in her seat. She would just wait and see what Mrs. Nicks had in mind this time.

The grumbling didn't seem to bother Mrs. Nicks. She was still smiling as she said, "Remember when we talked about the homeless people in our town? And how lonely they must feel just before Thanksgiving?"

Everyone nodded. Well, everyone except Duncan Fairbush. His blond head didn't move an inch. Caroline guessed he wasn't even listening.

But Caroline was interested. When she thought of Thanksgiving, she thought of turkey and pumpkin pie. But homeless people didn't have anything special to look forward to in the next three weeks. Thanksgiving would be like any other day to them.

"Here at Hart Elementary we're going to have an all-day costume fair a week from Friday," Mrs. Nicks said.

"Will there be prizes?" someone asked.

"Of course. There will be a prize for the best costume in each grade," the teacher told them.

Caroline immediately tried to think of something really wonderful to wear. For Halloween she had been a bunch of grapes, with purple balloons taped to a black leotard. But everyone had seen that costume. She would need something new.

Samantha Collins raised her hand. "What do

costumes and prizes have to do with the homeless?"

"In addition to the costumes," Mrs. Nicks explained, "each class will sponsor a booth. The money we earn will be donated to the shelter in Homestead. We'll have fun and help the homeless at the same time."

Maria Santiago winked at Caroline. It was her way of saying silently that she thought something sounded good. Caroline winked back at her best friend. She liked the idea, too. She could see herself dressed in a super costume, standing behind a counter collecting lots of money.

"What kind of booth will our class have?" Michael Hopkins asked from the back of the room. Caroline thought he was the neatest guy in the whole third grade.

Mrs. Nicks shook her head. "I'm not going to tell you what kind of booth to have. Each class has to decide for themselves what they want to sell. And they will design their own booth."

Caroline and Maria grinned at each other. Mrs. Nicks had been right. This *was* great news. It was going to be a lot of fun.

3

The teacher rubbed her hands together as if she was ready to get to work. "Let's decide what we'd like to do with our booth. What can we do to raise some money?" She sat on the edge of her desk and waited for people to make suggestions.

"We could sell raffle tickets . . . "

"My dad can give us the prize," Samantha said. "A stuffed dog from his toy store."

Caroline thought that it must be nice to have a dad who owned a toy store. But she wouldn't trade her own Grandpa Nevelson and his candy store for anybody in the world.

Next to her, Maria raised her hand. She pointed to the ribboned barrette in her hair. "My mother and I make these. We could sell them."

Duncan made a gagging sound.

"That's *girl* stuff," Michael told her. "What about a game?"

"What kind of game?" Mrs. Nicks asked him.

Michael thought for a minute before he decided, "One where you throw rings over something and you win a prize if your ring stays on."

Mrs. Nicks scribbled notes on a pad of paper.

"That sounds like an idea that might work. But we would need prizes to give away to the winners."

Caroline sucked on her bottom lip and thought hard. She tried to see the fair in her mind. In her head, she saw booths set up along the walls in the school gym. And kids were everywhere. Some were playing games. Others were looking hot and hungry.

That was it! Food! They should sell something for people to eat. Caroline held her hand high over her head.

"Do you have an idea, Caroline?" Mrs. Nicks asked.

"I think we should sell food . . . like a snack. My grandfather has a candy store and he would give us some stuff."

"Ooh . . . " Everybody sounded very interested in her idea.

But Mrs. Nicks shook her head. "Snacks are a good idea. But I don't think the parents would appreciate us selling candy."

Caroline tried to think fast. What else did she like to eat? "Cookies!" she called out. "We could sell home-baked cookies."

Mrs. Nicks finished scribbling on her note

pad. "If each of you brings just a dozen home-baked cookies, we will have more than three hundred of them to sell."

She sounded very pleased with the idea, and Caroline smiled so hard that her face hurt. She had been waiting since the beginning of September for her teacher to like one of her ideas.

"We could sell apples," Randy said from the far corner. His father owned a grocery store.

"I think we have enough suggestions," Mrs. Nicks said. Caroline grinned to herself. It was clear Mrs. Nicks did not like Randy's idea nearly as much as the cookie sale. She already knew what kind of cookies she would bake. Peanut butter-banana-marshmallow-surprise —the Zucker family favorite!

"I count five ideas." Mrs. Nicks's pencil touched the paper five times as she read, "A raffle with a big stuffed animal prize. Selling fancy barrettes. Selling apples. Selling home-baked cookies. Or a ring toss. Are you ready to vote?"

Samantha was the only one to vote for the raffle. No one voted for the barrettes, not even Maria. Randy raised his hand for the apples.

Caroline's heart pounded double-time when

it seemed like half the class voted for the cookies.

Finally, Mrs. Nicks asked those who liked the ring-toss idea to raise their hands. Slowly, the teacher counted all the hands waving in the air. "It's a tie between the cookies and the ring-toss. We'll vote again."

Lots of kids voted for Caroline's idea. But she worried when so many hands were raised for the ring-toss idea, too.

Mrs. Nicks looked confused. "This isn't right," she told the class. "We have twenty-seven students in class today. But I keep getting a tie when I count the votes. Thirteen of you want the cookies. And thirteen of you want the game. Who isn't voting?"

In front of Caroline, Duncan Fairbush raised his hand.

"Is there a reason you didn't vote?" Mrs. Nicks asked him.

"I couldn't decide."

Mrs. Nicks tried to sound patient when she asked, "Do you know now how you want to vote?"

Duncan bobbed his head up and down. "Yes, I do. I want the . . . "

Caroline covered her ears. She didn't want to hear him ruin her plan to impress the teacher.

"The ring-toss," he announced.

"That does it," Mrs. Nicks told the class. "Start thinking of what we can use for the booth and what kinds of prizes we will give our winners. Now it's time for social studies. Let's all turn to chapter five."

"Thanks for nothing," Caroline whispered to Duncan.

He peered over his shoulder. "I had to do it, Zucker. What if I bought a cookie you baked? I could die from it!"

Caroline decided she could still impress Mrs. Nicks. Instead of getting her social studies book out of her desk, she wildly waved her hand. Mrs. Nicks frowned. "Caroline? Is something wrong?"

"I still want to sell cookies at our booth."

"But we voted to have the ring-toss," Mrs. Nicks told her.

"Couldn't I sell cookies on the side?" she asked. "I'll make all of them." Mrs. Nicks's eyes opened wide in surprise and Caroline knew she was really impressing her.

8

"Are you sure?" the teacher wanted to know.

Caroline grinned and told her, "No problem. I'll bring ten batches."

Mrs. Nicks would *really* be amazed when she brought ten batches of peanut butter-banana-marshmallow-surprise to the fair!

2

THE SECRET MISSION

"What should we be for the costume fair?" Maria asked her mother the next afternoon. Mrs. Santiago designed costumes for the local theater, so she was sure to have lots of good ideas.

"What if we were twins?" Caroline asked. Then she glanced at Maria and realized it would be hard to make them look alike. Maria had long, wavy black hair. But Caroline's hair was light brown and straight and it didn't quite reach her shoulders, not even when she tried to stretch it.

"Twins aren't very exciting," Mrs. Santiago

told them. "What about being a horse? I could borrow a costume from the theater."

"But who wants to be the back half of a horse?" Caroline asked. She could just imagine the kind of jokes Duncan would make if she came to school as half a horse.

"Just one of us could be the horse," Maria said. "The other could be Paul Revere."

Caroline didn't want to be either the horse or Paul Revere. But then she started thinking about what they had been learning in social studies. Suddenly she had the perfect idea. "We can be Betsy Ross and the flag!"

Maria clapped her hands. "Yes!"

"That sounds like fun," Mrs. Santiago said.

"I want to be the flag," Caroline told her friend.

Maria frowned. "So do I."

Caroline squinted as she tried to imagine herself as the flag with thirteen stars. She could see herself *holding* a flag, but *being* a flag was a whole different thing. Maybe it would be better if Maria was the flag. After all, she was going to be an actress when she grew up.

"You can be the flag," Caroline told her friend.

11

"Really?" Maria smiled. "Are you sure you want to be Betsy Ross?"

"Sure." Caroline couldn't get too excited over playing a flag-sewer, but she didn't want to argue with Maria, either.

"We're going to win the prize for the best costume in the whole third grade!"

"Do you want me to help you with your costumes?" Mrs. Santiago asked.

"Yes!" both girls cried.

"I thought you might. What if I have sketches ready tomorrow afternoon? Can you come home with Maria after school again?" she asked Caroline.

"Sure." Her mom didn't mind how much time she spent at Maria's house as long as she didn't make a pest of herself.

With the costume problem solved, Maria started toward the kitchen. "Time for Double Club," she called over her shoulder.

Double Club was their own private idea. They had made it up because they couldn't join the Blue Jay Club at school until they were fourth graders.

Caroline poured lemonade into glasses full of ice while Maria found a pack of powdered sugar mini-doughnuts in the cupboard. But before Maria sat down at the glass-topped table, she grabbed a napkin and tucked it inside her collar.

"I don't want to get the powdered sugar all over my new sweater," she explained.

Caroline glanced down at her own boring jeans and navy blue turtleneck.

"It doesn't matter if I spill anything on my clothes," she told her friend.

"I know," Maria said sadly. "Your mom only buys you dark, plain clothes that are easy to wash. You would look so cute in my pale yellow sweater."

"The one with the butterflies on the shoulder?" Caroline would have given almost anything to have fun clothes like her friend.

"It's not fair. How is anyone supposed to know how great you are when you look so boring?" Maria asked.

Caroline made a face and tried to look very un-boring.

"That's not what I meant." Maria sighed.

"I know." Caroline sighed, too. "Sometimes I feel like there's a really fun, exciting person hiding underneath all my dumb dark clothes.

I've been trying to convince my mom I need pretty clothes ever since first grade."

"How? Have you ever made a real plan?"

Caroline shook her head.

"When you wanted to make Duncan Fairbush sorry he had been so mean, you had all kinds of plans and ideas." Maria ate a doughnut. "How is this any different?"

"Maybe it's not." Caroline realized she had never really planned a way to convince her mother to change her mind.

"Ooh . . . " Maria sat on the edge of her chair. "I can see the light in your eyes. You have an idea, don't you?"

"Just the beginning of a plan," Caroline said. "My mom is tired of hearing me argue about my clothes. What if we fix it so she figures out for herself that I need some fun new outfits?"

"What will we have to do?"

Caroline scratched her head. "It's not going to be easy. We'll have to figure out the plan as it happens." With her friend's help, Caroline started to believe things could really change. "I'll be a whole new person by Christmas."

"*Christmas?* Why wait so long?" Maria asked, her dark eyes sparkling. "By Thanksgiving."

"That's in three weeks!" Caroline wasn't sure any plan could work so fast.

"But think about the exciting Caroline Zucker trapped inside your old clothes," Maria told her. "She doesn't want to stay there until Christmas. You have to let her out!"

Caroline pushed her long sleeves up to her elbows. "You're right. I'll start working on my plan right away."

"When?" Maria whispered as if they were talking about some secret mission.

Caroline leaned across the kitchen table and whispered, "Tonight!"

"This is it!" Caroline cried. She had sneaked the newspaper up to her room after dinner and now she could barely believe her good luck. She hadn't been checking the paper for more than five minutes when she found the answer to her problem. Bernard's, the biggest department store in town, was having a huge one-day sale, including kids' clothes.

The newspaper was opened wide across her pink-and-white checked bedspread. Caroline hugged her knees to her chest and stared at the half-page advertisement. How could she make

15

her mother think it was her own idea to buy her pretty clothes?

Caroline remembered that on her mother's last birthday, Mrs. Zucker had wanted a cordless phone. She had left catalogs all over the house for Mr. Zucker—even on his breakfast plate. Then, when her mother had started working full-time as a nurse at the hospital, her father had gotten tired of the family never seeing each other. So he had tucked a newspaper article about family council meetings under Mrs. Zucker's fork. In both cases, the plan had worked.

Caroline knew exactly what to do with the Bernard's advertisement. She would leave it on her mother's chair at the kitchen table. If it worked, she'd go shopping with her mom tomorrow night!

Caroline wished she could talk to someone about her plan. But since it had to be a secret, she couldn't tell her sisters. And she couldn't even call Maria, because someone in the house might hear what she was saying.

Caroline looked at the fishbowl across the room. "Secrets can be a pain, Justin and Esmerelda," she told her fish. "And trying to put an idea into someone else's head is hard work."

Getting back to her project, she cut the page with the ad out of the paper and folded it down the center. One side showed the ad, and the other had three articles on it. She folded it a second time, so the only thing showing was the Bernard's advertisement.

Once everybody was in bed, she would grab her flashlight, tiptoe down to the kitchen, and put the ad on her mother's chair. Caroline crossed her fingers and winked at her goldfish. "Wish me luck!"

3

ONE OF THE GUYS

"Caroline, what are you doing?" Her father's deep voice seemed to bounce off the kitchen cupboards the next morning.

"I'm just putting some jelly on my toast," she said.

"Are you sure you're not just putting a piece of toast under your jelly?" he teased.

When Caroline looked down at her plate, she giggled. She had been so busy watching her mom that she hadn't noticed the strawberry jelly was nearly an inch thick on her bread.

"I don't have that much jelly," Caroline's six-year-old sister Patricia complained.

"I *like* jelly," her littlest sister Vicki said.

"You can have some of mine," Caroline told her. She scooped half her strawberry goo onto Vicki's plate.

"That's *disgusting,*" Patricia said, using her favorite word of the month.

"What's this?" Mrs. Zucker reached for the newspaper on her chair.

"Looks like a newspaper clipping to me," Caroline's father said.

"What are you trying to tell me this time?" Mrs. Zucker asked him.

"It's not from me," he said, sounding very innocent.

"Of course not . . . " Mrs. Zucker sat in her chair and unfolded the paper.

Caroline held her breath while her mother glanced over it. First, she read quickly through the articles. Next, she glanced at the Bernard's ad.

"I said, *please pass the milk,*" Patricia shouted.

"Sorry." Caroline hadn't heard her sister's first request. She handed the milk carton to Patricia, never taking her eyes off her mother.

"Bernard's has shoes on sale," Mrs. Zucker

said at last. "I could use a new pair. I'm on my feet so much at the hospital that I need to be comfortable."

"Wasn't it nice of someone to let you know about the shoe sale?" Mr. Zucker asked.

"Don't think you've fooled me," Mrs. Zucker said, smiling. She tucked the Bernard's ad into her pocket, but Caroline knew it was just so she'd remember to buy new shoes. Her first plan had failed, but she wasn't going to give up hope.

All she had to do was think of the next step in her plan to free the new and improved Caroline Zucker hiding under her ugly green Hart Elementary T-shirt.

"This group is organizing the prizes, right?" Mrs. Nicks asked the four students who had pulled their desks into a circle. "What's your plan?"

Maria spoke up first. "Caroline wrote it all down. She should tell you."

Caroline had to speak loudly to be heard. Different groups were doing different things, and all of them were noisy.

"We've decided on four kinds of prizes. Peo-

21

ple will get three rings for a quarter. If someone gets one ring on a peg, they get a prize from the first group—"

"An apple or orange," Randy interrupted.

"Or candy," Caroline added. "If someone gets two rings on the pegs, their prize comes from the second group—a barrette or a small toy. Some people might get all three rings on pegs. They should get a better prize."

"What might that be?" Mrs. Nicks asked.

"My dad said he could give us a lot of toys and stuff," Samantha said.

"Did you say there was a fourth category?" asked the teacher.

"Yes. We thought there should be a special prize if anyone got all three rings on the *same* peg," Caroline said.

"Then this group will have to decide later what that special prize will be." Mrs. Nicks smiled at Caroline. "You've all done a very good job."

"Hey, Caroline," Michael Hopkins called from the back of the room. "Can you help me?"

A big plastic tablecloth covered the floor in the farthest corner where some boys were painting big wooden pegs. Michael was in another corner where a huge piece of plywood was balanced against the wall.

But Caroline didn't see Michael, just two boys holding the board. "Where are you, Michael?"

"Back here." He stuck his head around the edge of the wood. "This board is the bottom of our booth. I'm marking where the pegs will go." He pointed to a small X on her side of the board. "We'll put a peg here. We'll be hammering the nails from back here. And we have to know the nails will hit the pegs."

"What do I do?"

"Hammer a small nail through each mark in the front of the board. I'll watch from the back to make sure the nails come through in the right places."

"Hammer? You want me to *hammer?*" Who did he think she was? One of the guys?

Caroline glanced at the other groups. Maria and their friends were still discussing the prizes. Several girls were working on the booth sign. They had covered their pretty clothes with their art shirts.

"Something wrong?" Michael asked her.

A lot of things were wrong. But they weren't

things she could tell Michael Hopkins. Instead, she said only, "I don't know much about hammering."

One of the boys holding the board said, "You're the only one who can do it. All the other guys are full of paint."

"Maybe you could do the hammering, and I could stand behind the board and watch for the nails to come through," she said.

Michael just pointed to the hammer and nails on a desk and disappeared behind the board again.

"I'm ready," he called.

Caroline held the nail in the center of the first X. She closed one eye and hit the nail gently with the hammer.

"Harder," Michael told her.

Wondering if he would have asked her to help him if she'd been wearing a cute little pink dress, Caroline hit the nail . . . hard. It wasn't that she wanted the guys to think she was helpless, but why couldn't they notice she was a *girl?*

"Perfect!" Michael said. She was about to thank him when he added, "We marked this one just right."

After she had helped them check all the spots where the pegs would go, the boys got ready to paint red X's over the smaller marks. When no one asked her to help with the painting, Caroline decided to talk to Maria. She passed Mrs. Nicks on her way to the front of the room.

"It looked like you did a good job back there," the teacher said. "You're a very good sport."

Caroline was surprised by Mrs. Nicks's compliment. The teacher was squinting at her yellow notepad.

"Are you still planning to bring ten batches of cookies to sell at the booth?" she asked.

Caroline liked being called a good sport. She grinned at her teacher. "Of course I'll bring them!"

4

A NEW CAROLINE

"I hope you don't mind about my sisters," Caroline told Maria Saturday morning. Before her friend could answer, Patricia and Vicki trotted into the Santiago house.

"My mom will have fun designing four costumes for the fair," Maria said.

"But they don't even know what they want to be," Caroline whispered. "Your mom won't have any time left to help us."

"Welcome, welcome." Mrs. Santiago took the girls' jackets and hung them in the closet. "I thought we could all work in my studio." Maria's mother had an office at home and children were very rarely allowed inside it. Caroline realized this was a special day.

"This is the first part of your costume," she told Caroline as the group marched into her studio. "It's the sort of thing a girl in Betsy Ross's time wore under her dress." She dropped a cream-colored shift over Caroline's head. "You'll need to sew this part and then your shift will be finished."

"Sew it?" It had taken Caroline half an hour to sew a button on her blouse last week.

"I can use the sewing machine," Maria told her. "I'll do it for you."

While Caroline watched Maria stitch the side seams, Mrs. Santiago talked with Patricia and Vicki.

"I want something pretty," Patricia insisted. "I want to be a princess."

"A princess." Mrs. Santiago glanced at Maria. "Maria, would you get that blue dress you wore in the school play two years ago?"

Maria pushed back her chair and said, "No problem. I hate that old thing."

She hurried out of the room and returned with a long, blue velvet dress on a hanger.

"It's beautiful," Patricia sighed.

27

"Try it on, honey," Mrs. Santiago said.

Patricia couldn't wait to get into it. "It's so nice." She turned a slow circle and asked, "How do I look?"

Mrs. Santiago took a few steps back to get a good look. "I think it fits you very well. If we add some lace and pearls, you'll be a real princess."

"Pearls?" Patricia swallowed hard.

"And of course, you'll need a golden crown."

"A golden crown," Patricia echoed dreamily.

"Maybe when your mom sees how great Patricia looks she'll realize you need pretty clothes, too," Maria suggested to Caroline as she finished the last seam.

"Maybe. It's hard to tell what will convince my mom." Caroline took off her clothes and left them in a heap on the floor. Then she slipped into the shift.

"What's next, Mrs. Santiago?" she asked.

Maria's mother held up a dress made of soft green material. "Just as I thought." She smiled. "This color makes your eyes come alive. A child wore it in a play we did last year."

Caroline wished she could see for herself.

28

Maybe it wasn't going to be so boring being Betsy Ross after all.

"It goes over your shift," she explained, helping Caroline put the dress on. The skirt was open in the front to show the underskirt. Mrs. Santiago fussed with the green dress, getting it just right. "All you need is a sash to tie around your waist. And your cap." She pulled something white out of a box. "I found this at the theater last night."

"It looks like a shower cap!" Patricia said with a laugh.

"It looks like what the grandmother wears on her head in my *Little Red Riding Hood* book!" Vicki said.

Mrs. Santiago smiled. "You're both right. But it's what all the women wore back in Betsy Ross's time."

She slipped the ruffled cap over Caroline's head. Then she pulled out some hair on each side of her face.

Mrs. Santiago handed Caroline a mirror as she said, "Try to imagine your hair is curled."

"I like it!" Caroline hardly recognized herself. The green overdress did look nice. Her eyes were sparkling, and all her straight brown hair was stuffed inside the cap. If Mrs. Santiago could get those little pieces on each side to curl, she would actually look pretty.

Vicki started jumping up and down. "What about me?"

Mrs. Santiago squatted so she could be face to face with Caroline's youngest sister. "Do you want to be a princess, too?"

"No." Vicki stuck out her bottom lip. "I want to be Little Pillow."

"Little Pillow?" Maria's mother sounded confused.

Caroline realized help was needed. "Little Pillow is an old pillow that Vicki has had since she was a baby. It leaves feathers behind wherever she takes it."

"Is it a special little pillow with baby ducks on it or anything like that?" Mrs. Santiago asked.

"No. It's just a dirty white pillow with pink stripes on it—and holes in it." Caroline wondered how Maria's mother was going to make Vicki into a walking Little Pillow.

Mrs. Santiago cleared a stack of papers off an old trunk. Then she flipped open the lid and almost disappeared inside as she looked for something. She rocked back on her heels and pulled out a piece of striped material.

"Does Little Pillow look anything like this?" she asked Vicki.

"Yes!" Vicki ran across the room and hugged the pink and white fabric.

"Then we'll make it into a big sack that you can wear. We'll find something to stuff it with, and then I'll get some feathers that we can glue to the outside so you'll look as if you're shedding!"

"That would be perfect," Caroline cried.

Vicki smiled one of her biggest smiles.

"What about Maria?" Caroline asked. They hadn't seen any part of her flag costume yet.

"We have to sew all the stripes together," Maria explained. "But it's going to be really neat."

"Do you girls need something?" Mrs. Santiago asked Caroline and Maria after Patricia and Vicki had gone home.

Maria hurried to explain. "Caroline is tired of the way she looks. She thinks she looks like a boy. Could you help her?"

"I think we might be able to do something."

Mrs. Santiago ran her fingers through Caroline's fine, brown hair. "Let's start by styling her hair."

Before she knew what was happening, Caroline's head was bent over the bathroom sink. Mrs. Santiago shampooed her hair. When she finished, she wrapped a towel around Caroline's head.

Then she sprayed some mousse into her palm, rubbed her hands together, and fluffed the mousse through Caroline's hair.

"What will this do?" Caroline hoped her hair wouldn't turn green or anything. How would she explain that to her mother?

"It will give your hair some body," Mrs. Santiago told her. "We don't want it to look so flat."

Next, Maria's mother used the blow dryer. When Caroline's hair was almost dry, Mrs. Santiago used a round brush on her bangs and on the ends. When she finished, Caroline had to look into the mirror twice. Was that really her?

"What do you think?" Mrs. Santiago asked.

Carefully, Caroline touched her hair. It puffed out just a little on the sides, and then it curved under at the bottom. She really liked how she looked.

"What about her clothes?" Maria asked. "She doesn't look like a boy anymore. Now she looks like a girl wearing boys' clothes."

Mrs. Santiago stared at the two girls standing next to each other. "Maria, you're just a little taller than Caroline. Do you have any dresses that are too small for you?"

"Sure. And I know just the one for Caroline to try."

Caroline followed Maria down the hall to her friend's bedroom and waited while Maria searched in her closet.

"This is the one." Maria showed her a dress. The top was pink with black polka dots. The bottom half was a pink skirt with two pink-and-black polka dot ruffles. "Do you want to try it on?"

"Of course!" Caroline took off her ugly, dark clothes.

Together, they got the dress over Caroline's head without damaging her new hair. Caroline twirled in circles in the middle of Maria's room. It was a wonderful dress. She loved the way the ruffles fluttered when she spun around.

"What would my mom say if she saw me like this?" she asked her friend.

"Why don't you wear it home?" Mrs. Santiago said from the open doorway. "You look darling."

Darling. That was a word people used when they described sweet little Vicki. Caroline wasn't sure she had ever been called *darling* in her whole life.

The grandfather clock in the living room chimed. Caroline's mouth fell open. "It's six o'clock! I'm supposed to be home right now."

"No problem." Mrs. Santiago jangled her keys in her pocket. "I can drive you."

Caroline could hardly wait to get home. She wanted her mother to notice she was growing up. Then they could have a nice talk about clothes and other things.

She waved to Mrs. Santiago before she opened the front door to her house. Piano scales greeted Caroline as she stepped inside.

"What happened to you?" Patricia asked, hopping off the piano bench.

"Boy, do you look silly!" Vicki giggled.

34

Caroline's mom came into the living room and smiled. "Isn't that cute! Were you girls playing dress-up?"

Caroline felt her face getting hot. What was the matter with everybody? *Playing dress-up?* She wasn't playing anything. She was dressed like a real third-grade girl.

Without answering or looking at anyone, Caroline ran past them and rushed upstairs to her room. She managed to hold back the tears until her door was shut behind her. Then she fell across her bed and cried.

5

THE PRINCESS AND LITTLE PILLOW

"Maria!" Vicki and Patricia screamed Monday afternoon. They nearly knocked the box she was carrying out of her hands when she came into the house. They knew Maria had come to help them with their costumes.

Maria set her box on the floor and put a yellow folder on top of it. Vicki was jumping up and down with excitement. Maria asked, "Do you want to see how my mother drew you as Little Pillow?"

"Oh, yes!"

"What about me?" Patricia wanted to know.

36

Maria said, "Just wait a minute, okay? I have something for you, too."

"What's going on?" Laurie Morrell, the high-school girl who stayed at the Zucker house until one of the girls' parents got home, came out of the kitchen.

"Costumes," Patricia said.

"Maria has pictures." Vicki was still grinning as she took Maria's hand. "Come and show me Little Pillow."

Caroline picked up the box as the others started tromping into the family room. The box was very light. She wondered what could be inside.

When Caroline came into the family room, Maria opened her folder and took out a sheet of paper. "This is how you will look as Little Pillow," she told Vicki.

Vicki's face lit up as she peered at the paper. Then she looked up at Maria. "This is me?"

Maria nodded. Caroline was dying to see how Mrs. Santiago was going to turn her little sister into a pillow. She looked down at the drawing, too.

The sack that made the pillow reached from Vicki's neck to her knees. There were small rips in the white material with pink stripes, and feathers were poking through the holes.

"My mom wants to know if you like the idea," Maria told Vicki. "She can make the costume, if you like it."

"I love it." Vicki gently touched the drawing. "I'm going to *be* Little Pillow!"

"That's great, but what about me?" Patricia asked. "Do you have a princess picture? I want to show Laurie how I'm going to look."

"No picture for you." Maria pointed to the box. "But check in there."

Patricia ripped the box open. Then she peeked inside. "Ooh . . . "

"Take it out," Maria told her.

Carefully, Patricia lifted a golden crown out of the box. It was made of cardboard sprayed gold, but it looked real to Caroline.

Patricia put it on her head.

"It's beautiful," Laurie said.

Vicki puckered her lips and sniffed.

"What's wrong?" Caroline asked.

"Maybe I want to be a princess, too."

Laurie picked up Vicki and gave her a hug. "You're going to be wonderful as Little Pillow. No one else will have a costume that special."

Vicki rubbed her nose and sniffed just once more. Then she smiled at Laurie and said, "Okay."

Maria seemed to be looking for something in the box. Then she held up a sparkling plastic bag in her hand.

"The crown isn't finished yet," she told Patricia. "My mom sent you these sequins and other shiny things to glue onto it."

"I can't wait to start," Patricia cried.

"Maybe you should let someone help you," Laurie suggested. "Wait for your mom. She's coming home before dinner tonight."

"Mommy's coming home soon?" Vicki ran to the window to look for their mother's red car.

Laurie checked her watch. "She should be on her way home right now. I'd better finish chopping those vegetables."

Vicki stayed at the window with her nose pressed against the glass. Patricia started dancing around the family room in her crown.

"Want to see what my costume will look like?" Maria asked Caroline. She pulled another paper out of her folder. In the drawing, Maria was standing with her arms stretched out on each side. The flag costume covered all

40

of her. Only her head, her hands, and some of her legs showed. The blue square with thirteen stars reached from her right wrist to somewhere near her right armpit. All the rest of her was red and white stripes.

"Are you going to walk around all day with your arms sticking out?" Caroline asked.

"Only when someone wants to know what I'm supposed to be," Maria told her. "But when I drop my arms, I look like some strange kind of bird with red and white wings."

Caroline giggled.

"Did you notice the stars?" Maria asked suddenly.

"Sure. There are thirteen."

Maria pointed to a star near her wrist in the drawing. "Look at this one."

Bringing the paper closer, Caroline noticed it was different. "It looks like it's falling off."

"That's right! My mom is going to leave a thread and needle hanging from it. Whenever you want to, you can pretend you are really sewing the stars on the flag!"

Caroline was speechless. Mrs. Santiago was so clever! No one was going to have a costume like hers and Maria's.

"Girls," Laurie called from the kitchen. "Could I get some help?"

"Sure." Both Caroline and Maria rushed into the next room.

"I have to finish cutting up vegetables for the salad, but I also have to put some muffins into the oven." Laurie pointed toward a bowl on the counter. "You don't have to do much. I've already stirred the batter. If you could just mix in the blueberries and then fill the muffin tins . . . "

Caroline had the blueberries in her hand before Laurie could finish her instructions. She let the berries drop into the batter one by one. Then Laurie handed Maria two greased muffin pans to be filled.

They had just scooped the last of the batter into the last muffin cup when Mrs. Zucker came in the back door.

"We're making muffins," Caroline told her.

Mrs. Zucker checked their work and nodded. "Good work, ladies. You're certainly looking very nice today, Maria."

"Thank you, Mrs. Zucker. Do you like my new blouse?" Maria tucked her white blouse with the pale blue flowers on it into her jeans.

"Just look at it, Mom." Caroline thought she'd found the perfect time to make a point about her clothes. "It's light colors and Maria kept it clean all day. Even while we made muffins!"

Mrs. Zucker smiled. "But Caroline, you are not Maria."

"Mom!" Vicki ran into the kitchen and grabbed her mother and the clothes discussion was finished.

"Come here," Caroline whispered to Maria. As they headed upstairs to her bedroom, she told her friend, "Time for an emergency Double Club meeting."

"I know," Maria said.

They collapsed on the bed. Caroline sighed loudly. "I can't stand it. She'll *never* buy me any pretty clothes. I'll still be wearing jeans and dark shirts when I get to Aspen Middle School!"

"I've got it!" Maria snapped her fingers. "I'll bring you an outfit tomorrow. You can bring it home and then wear it to school on Wednesday! Your mom won't mind because they won't be your clothes!"

"Which outfit?" Caroline scooted closer to

her friend so they could plan their next move. "I like your pink shirt and pants—the ones where the checks show on the bottom of the pant legs if you turn up the cuff."

Maria lifted her right palm and Caroline slapped her hand against it. They had a deal. Who could have a better friend?

6

PINK FINGERNAILS

"What's this for?" Caroline picked up a small bottle in her parents' bedroom Monday night.

"It's cream to keep my eyes from looking puffy," her mother explained.

Caroline picked up a strange silver thing. "And this?"

"An eyelash curler." Mrs. Zucker sat on the edge of her bed. "What are all the questions for?"

Instead of answering, Caroline asked another one. "When can I get my ears pierced?"

Her mother sighed. "Honey, we've had this

conversation before. When you're in middle school."

That wouldn't be for *three years.* "You know, Mom, I'm not a little kid anymore."

Mrs. Zucker nodded as if she understood. But Caroline knew her mother did not understand because she still didn't have clothes like the other girls in third grade. Somehow, Caroline had to think of a way to start making some changes. Then she saw her mother's collection of nail polishes. "Could I polish my nails tonight?" Everyone would notice if she had bright red nails at school tomorrow.

"Sure." Her mother started moving nail polish bottles around as if she was looking for something special. "This one should do it."

It wasn't bright red, but Caroline didn't mind. It was a very light pink, just like the outfit she was going to borrow from Maria. Day after next, her fingers were going to match her clothes!

Caroline took the bottle in her clasped hands. "It's perfect!"

She ran upstairs to her bedroom and shut the door so no one would bother her and began painting her nails. They were very short. Until now, it hadn't mattered that she chewed them when she got nervous.

"This growing up stuff isn't easy," she told her goldfish. As if they understood her, both Justin and Esmerelda swam closer to her.

"I'm not sure my mom is ever going to let me dress like the other girls," she told them sadly. "But I'm tired of the guys thinking I'm one of them. No one is going to ask me to hammer nails tomorrow!"

"You know, your nails are lumpy," Patricia said as soon as the three girls were out the door the next morning.

"Don't make fun. Caroline's hands look pretty." Vicki cuddled close to her oldest sister.

Caroline glanced at her fingers in the morning sunlight. So what if her nails weren't perfect? It was her first time using actual polish. The stuff in the little girl makeup sets didn't really count. She was determined not to let Patricia spoil her morning. Today, she would surprise everyone with her pink nails and the pink bow clipped in her hair. Tomorrow they would probably faint when they saw her in Maria's outfit.

She touched the bow on top of her head. Instead of parting her hair down the center, she had brushed it back and then clipped it with a pink ribbon.

"Where did you get the pretty bow?" Vicki asked.

Before Caroline could answer, Patricia spoke for her. "Grandpa Nevelson gave it to you for Christmas. Right?"

"Right." Sometimes Caroline believed their grandfather was the only person who understood the Zucker girls.

"Why do you want pink fingernails?" Patricia asked as they turned the corner toward Hart Elementary.

"I just want to look more grown-up. More . . . " Caroline tried to find just the right word and chose the one that people often used to describe Maria. "More feminine."

"What's that?" Vicki wrinkled her nose.

Caroline touched her pink bow again to make sure it hadn't slipped or anything. "More feminine means looking more like a girl."

"But you *are* a girl," Vicki said. "We all are!"

Caroline pointed to some of the other kids walking up the sidewalk to the school's front door. "See Samantha Collins? And that little red-haired girl in the purple skirt? Some girls look more like girls than I do."

Patricia looked at Caroline's dark green jeans and T-shirt. "Yeah. What are you going to do about it?"

"I'm working on a plan," Caroline told her sisters. Suddenly, it seemed more important than ever to convince their mother to let her wear pretty clothes.

"You're gonna die when you see my gorilla costume," Tim announced to anyone who would listen as the class worked on their fair booth that afternoon.

"I bet you'll scare all the girls," Duncan said.

Caroline checked her pink fingernails. She might look more feminine, but she wasn't going to be afraid of Tim in a gorilla suit. What a dumb idea!

"Ooh . . . " Maria tugged on Caroline's arm. "Look."

The sign-painting team was showing off their work. In bright red letters, it announced: *Nicks's Ring-Toss.* The game had been named in honor of their teacher.

"Who wants to help nail it to the front of the booth?" Michael asked. He glanced in Caroline's direction, but she shook her head.

"Let's work on the prize baskets," Maria said. "They need to be painted. And we have to make labels."

"Let's do labels and use your markers," Caroline suggested.

"I almost forgot!" Maria opened her desk and handed a brown bag to Caroline. She whispered, "It's the pink top and pants."

A tingle shot through Caroline's body all the way down to her toes as she stuffed the bag into her own desk. Tomorrow she was going to be the new-and-improved Caroline Zucker, and everyone was going to be amazed.

"Hey, Zucker!" Duncan Fairbush yelled from the back of the room. "What are you doing?"

"Making the signs for the prize baskets," Caroline told him.

He groaned. "You were boring before, Zucker, but now . . . " Instead of finishing that sentence, he said, "I think that dumb bow has turned your brain to mush."

Mush? Caroline wanted to jump out of her chair and punch Duncan Fairbush, but Maria grabbed her elbow. "Don't waste your energy on him."

Caroline took a deep breath and stayed in her seat.

"Listen, guys!" Duncan called to his friends. "It's amazing. Zucker has nothing to say!"

Maria slapped her marker packet on her desk. "My mother always says I should ignore people who act stupid. So let's ignore Duncan and work on our labels."

Duncan's friend Kevin Sutton told the boys, "I think she's just being quiet because she knows Duncan's going to win the prize for the best costume on Friday."

"Yeah." Duncan laughed. "Zucker *hates* to lose."

Caroline opened her mouth, and Maria kicked her under the table. "Don't say anything!" her friend whispered.

"You're right," Caroline answered. *"He's* the one who is going to be surprised on Friday when *we* win the prize!"

7

IT HAPPENS!

"What's this?" Mrs. Zucker asked as she sat on the family-room couch after dinner. She pulled a brown bag from under the orange couch pillow, and Caroline's throat went dry. It was the bag with Maria's clothes in it! How could she have forgotten it when she unpacked her school bag that afternoon?

Her mother opened the bag and pulled out the pink shirt. Caroline held her breath. As Mrs. Zucker took out the pink pants with their checked cuffs, Caroline clasped her hands behind her back.

"Do you know anything about this?" her mother asked.

Caroline looked over her shoulder to see if anyone else had come into the room, but her sisters were still clearing the dinner dishes off the table. There was no question about it. Her mother was talking to her.

"Maybe," she answered.

"What *might* you know?" Her mother didn't sound angry. Just curious.

"They're Maria's clothes." Caroline knew if she looked her mother right in the eye, the whole truth would come spilling out. And then her mother would sigh and say she had heard the whole clothes argument before, and that would be the end of it.

"Did Maria leave them here?" her mother asked.

"Not exactly."

Mrs. Zucker smoothed the wrinkles out of the pink pants and folded them. "These are cute. How did they get here, Caroline?"

"In my school bag."

"Does Maria know you have them?"

"Of course!" Caroline was shocked. Did her

53

mother think she'd stolen them? "She loaned them to me."

"Did she lend them to you for a reason? Does it have something to do with your costume for the fair?"

Caroline wished she could lie and say the clothes were part of her costume. But everyone knew Betsy Ross had never worn pink pants. She took a deep breath and decided to tell the whole story.

"I borrowed the outfit so I could wear it to school tomorrow. I wanted to know how it would feel to look feminine." Once she got started, it was hard to stop. "I wanted people to notice I'm a girl. I'm just so tired of looking like one of the boys . . . ."

Suddenly, Caroline's words could not get past the lump in her throat. She wanted her mom to understand how important this was to her. She wanted it so badly that she had a pain in her stomach.

Caroline peeked at her mother, expecting to find a don't-bother-me-with-this-again look on her face. But instead, Mrs. Zucker looked thoughtful.

"Do you really think you look like a boy?" she asked slowly.

"Last week Michael Hopkins and I were wearing the exact same turtleneck on the same day. And I was the only girl the boys asked to hammer nails for the fair booth."

"You didn't like that?"

"Maybe a little. But Mom, they didn't think any of the *other* girls should know about hammers and nails—just me," she explained.

Caroline's mother said, "And you think your clothes are the reason the boys treat you like one of them?"

"Yes!"

"How can clothes make that much difference?"

Caroline shrugged her shoulders. "They just do."

Mrs. Zucker was silent for a minute. She folded the pink shirt and laid it on top of the pants. Then she fluffed the orange couch pillow and put it behind her back.

Caroline was beginning to think the conversation was over, but she couldn't go upstairs and leave Maria's clothes on the couch. She cleared her throat to get her mother's attention. "Uh, Mom—can I wear the outfit to school tomorrow?"

"You really are growing up, aren't you?" Her mother stood and went over to Caroline. Then she wrapped her in a giant hug.

Happiness bubbled up in Caroline's heart and made her smile. Her mother finally understood!

Mrs. Zucker suddenly said, "Are you hungry?"

Hungry? "We just finished dinner."

"That doesn't matter," her mom said, leading Caroline into the kitchen. "Whenever my mother and I had important discussions, we *always* ate something."

Caroline waited while her mother rummaged through the refrigerator.

"How do you feel about applesauce?" Mrs. Zucker asked as she carried two bowls to the table.

"It's fine." Caroline would have been willing to eat liver if it meant they could finally talk about her problems.

Her mother made circles in the applesauce with her spoon. "Do I have this right, Caroline?

Is wearing dark shirts and pants keeping you from feeling pretty?"

"Yes!" Caroline didn't even bother to pick up her spoon. Eating would just distract her. "I don't feel pretty at all in my old clothes."

Her mother smiled, but it wasn't the kind of smile that meant she was laughing at Caroline. It was a smile that said she knew how Caroline felt.

"What can we do about it?" Mrs. Zucker asked.

"Go shopping?" Caroline suggested.

Mrs. Zucker nodded. "Shopping sounds like a good idea."

"Really?" Caroline nearly jumped out of her chair. "When?"

Her mother smiled. "I only have to work until four o'clock tomorrow. Do you have any plans for tomorrow evening?"

"Just practicing my spelling words, but that won't take very long. I'll do it when I get home from school so we can shop after dinner." Caroline was talking so fast that she had to stop and catch her breath.

Her mother ate some applesauce before she asked, "What do you want to buy?"

"They have some really cute sweat shirts at Kidstuff Boutique—Samantha has one. And I'd like one of those dresses with a ruffly skirt. I think I'd look great in light blue . . . "

Mrs. Zucker shook her head. "Not light blue. We should try mint green."

"Is that . . . " Caroline held her breath, hoping it wasn't a dark, boring green.

"Don't worry," her mother said. "It's a light green that will show off your brown hair and highlight your brown eyes."

Caroline touched her hair and checked that the pink bow was still in place. "A color can do all that?"

"And more." Her mother smiled. "It's going to be fun doing girl-things with you."

Closing her eyes, Caroline thought she had died and gone to heaven. Her mother wanted to do *girl-things* with her, like shopping for clothes that were her own special color! Under the table, she pinched her leg to make sure she wasn't dreaming.

There was a squeal from the living room, and Mrs. Zucker said, "What's going on?"

"Let's go see." Caroline pushed her chair

away from the table and raced in to the next room.

Vicki was spinning around in her Little Pillow suit while their father watched from the sofa. When she tried to bow, she couldn't make her fat costume bend in the middle. Everyone laughed.

"Here I am—Princess Patricia!" Caroline's other sister called from the hall. They all watched her sweep into the room. In her blue dress and golden crown, she really did look like a blond princess. She stood straight and held her head very high.

"Patricia . . . " Vicki's big brown eyes were huge. "You look *beautiful.*"

Patricia's lips turned up in a small, princess-like smile. Then she glanced at Caroline for a second. Caroline knew that Patricia was hoping her older sister would also compliment her, but she was afraid Caroline might just make a joke or tease her. "You do look pretty," Caroline told Patricia. "Like a real princess."

Patricia's princess-like smile turned into a wide grin.

Suddenly, Caroline wanted to be part of the

fashion show. She asked, "Will you guys wait for me to put on my costume?"

"If you hurry." Vicki patted a feather that was glued to one of the fake rips in her pillow suit.

Caroline raced up the stairs. She took her costume from the closet and climbed into the long shift. Then she pulled the green dress over her head. Checking the mirror, she tied the sash around her waist. Finally, she put the white cap on her head, tucking all her hair under it.

She almost tripped over her skirt as she hurried down the steps.

"I'm here," Caroline announced.

"It's Betsy Ross, right here in our house!" Mrs. Zucker said, pretending to be surprised.

"Miss Ross," her father said in his teacher's voice. "I've always wondered why you picked red, white and blue for the flag."

Caroline shook her finger at her father. "I'm glad you asked that question. I wanted to put some pink on the flag, but George made me use red."

"George?" Her mother raised her eyebrows.

"I think she means George Washington," Mr. Zucker explained.

Even though Vicki wasn't quite sure who George Washington was, she laughed along with the rest of the family. Her pillow suit jiggled like a bowl of Jell-O.

"Oh, Vicki," Caroline called. "You are *so* cute!"

Vicki grinned. "Do I have the best costume in the whole kindergarten? Will I win?"

Nodding her head, Caroline said, "You could."

In just two days one of them—or maybe all three of them—could be winning prizes for their costumes at the school fair. And in less than twenty-four hours she would be shopping with her mother to buy *girl* clothes!

There was only one problem. How was she going to wait until tomorrow night?

8

SHOPPING IS HARD WORK

Caroline closed the dressing room door at the Kidstuff Boutique on Wednesday night. Then she climbed out of Maria's pink pants and top and tried on a pair of white leggings.

"They fit nicely," her mother said from the corner of the small dressing room. Mrs. Zucker slipped a pale green shirt off its hanger. It was like an extra-long T-shirt. When Caroline put it on, it reached halfway to her knees.

"I love it," Caroline said. She thought the other girls at school looked great in this kind of outfit.

Her mother smiled. "You sure look different from the Caroline Zucker I used to know."

"Is that good?" Caroline held her breath. She thought the change was a good thing, but she hoped her mother would agree.

Mrs. Zucker said, "Yes. I think I like the new Caroline."

The NEW Caroline! It was exactly what she had wanted to be! The girls would crowd around, saying how much they loved her new clothes. And maybe Michael Hopkins would notice she was really a girl.

"Can I get it?" she asked her mother.

"If you want it, you know our deal," Mrs. Zucker said. "We're spending the money I'd been saving in my rainy day fund. When the money's gone, the shopping is over."

"Hmm . . . " Caroline thought about the hundreds of other outfits in the other stores at the mall. What if she bought the leggings and shirt, and then she found something she liked better?

"You can't decide?" asked her mother, the mind-reader. She handed Maria's pink clothes to Caroline. "While you put these back on, I'll ask the woman at the counter to hold the white pants and the green top. If we don't come back before the store closes, she'll know we decided not to buy them."

"You can do that?" It sounded too easy to Caroline.

"I do it all the time when I shop," her mother explained. "I can never make up my mind when I'm buying clothes."

Caroline giggled. She was just like her mother! They understood each other! Until now, she hadn't realized how much fun growing up could be.

"Do your feet hurt?" Caroline asked almost two hours later.

"No." Mrs. Zucker kept on walking at a quick pace. "I'm on my feet all the time at the hospital so they're pretty tough."

Caroline felt one of her bags falling. When she tried to hold on to it, her other packages started to slip out of her arms.

"I could carry some of those for you," her mother offered.

"I'm fine," Caroline said. She loved having her arms full of packages holding her bright, happy new clothes.

Her mother started taking smaller steps. "You're getting tired, aren't you?" she asked.

Caroline tried to nod, but one of the bags was caught under her chin. "Shopping is hard work."

"But you got some nice things. Which outfit will you wear tomorrow?" Mrs. Zucker asked.

The choices took turns popping into Caroline's thoughts. There were the white pants and the green top. But she also liked the jeans with the pleats at the waist. They looked great with the soft blue sweater they had found at Bernard's. The red jumpsuit with its shiny black belt was fun. And she loved the lavender dress with its flouncy skirt.

"I like them all so much." Caroline couldn't decide. "Maybe I'll wait and see what feels right in the morning."

"That's a very good idea."

A delicious smell tickled Caroline's nose as they passed the Chunky Chip Cookie Shop. "Oh, Mom, don't you need a cookie?"

Mrs. Zucker bought a cookie for each of them. They took their cookies and napkins to a bench in the center of the mall. Caroline set all her packages down before she took her first bite.

"Mmm . . . this is almost as good as the peanut butter-banana-marshmallow-surprise cookies that you . . . " Caroline stared at her mother. "Oh no!"

"What's wrong? Did you bite into something that doesn't belong in a cookie?" her mother asked.

Caroline shook her head. It was worse. Much worse. "I forgot. I promised to bring ten batches of homemade cookies to the fair. We're going to sell them at our booth!"

"But I thought your class was making a ring-toss game."

"The kids almost voted to have a cookie sale. Then Duncan voted for the ring-toss," Caroline said. "But Mrs. Nicks really liked my cookie idea. So I said I'd make all the cookies."

"Ten batches!" Mrs. Zucker shook her head. "It's already Wednesday night. You're going to be very busy tomorrow night."

Caroline stared at all the goodies in the Chunky Chip shop. "I have an idea," she told her mom. "We could *buy* the cookies."

"That's a good idea, but we just spent my

whole rainy day fund." Mrs. Zucker pulled two lonely dollar bills out of an envelope. "This is all I have left. It won't buy many cookies."

"How many supplies can it buy for peanut butter-banana-marshmallow-surprises?" Caroline asked.

"Don't worry," her mother said. "I can write a check at the grocery store. Spencer's is on our way home."

Luckily, Spencer's was open late. Caroline just hoped her mother knew how much stuff to buy to make ten batches of cookies.

"This is neat," Maria announced in the Zuckers' kitchen Thursday evening. "It's like a Double Club field trip." She was wearing one of her father's old shirts to keep her clothes clean.

Laurie Morrell handed Caroline an apron and Caroline put it on over her light blue sweater and new pleated jeans. Then she handed the ties to Laurie so the baby sitter could make a tight knot. Caroline was determined not to get flour or mashed bananas on her new clothes.

"I'm glad you're here," she told Laurie. "I

wanted to do it with my mom, but she had to work tonight."

Maria grinned. "Well, I'm glad your dad had a meeting at school. Can you imagine baking cookies with him in the kitchen?"

"Definitely not!" Laurie laughed when she thought about Mr. Zucker, her history teacher, working in the kitchen.

Suddenly, Maria poked Caroline in the side. She dropped her voice very low and said, "Hey, Zucker! What's with the sweater? It's not black."

Caroline loved her friend's imitation of Duncan. "He really was surprised to see me looking like the other girls . . . . "

"*Better* than the other girls," Maria corrected. "You looked super today."

Caroline grinned as she remembered how special she'd felt wearing her pretty new outfit. She'd even gotten compliments from some of her friends. It sure was fun being feminine!

Laurie tossed a huge bag of flour onto the kitchen counter. "Can you help me get the ingredients ready?"

"Sure." Maria helped Laurie and Caroline stack five bags of sugar, a dozen big jars of peanut butter and lots of bananas next to the flour. "Are we really going to use all this stuff?" She stared at the mountain of baking supplies.

Laurie scratched her head. "I hate to say it, Caroline, but we're never going to be able to make all these cookies in one night. We need more people."

"Who?" Caroline asked.

"What about your sisters?" Laurie suggested.

"Not them!" Caroline groaned. "They'll mess everything up!"

Laurie patted her shoulder. "I'm sorry, Caroline. But you really don't have a choice. I'll go get them."

9

SURPRISE, SURPRISE!

"Let's have teams," Vicki said, dragging a chair from the kitchen table to the counter.

"Yeah!" Patricia seemed to love the idea. "We can race!"

Vicki scrambled into the chair and stood on the seat so she was tall enough to see what was on the counter. "Wow! Are we making a million cookies?"

"Probably," Caroline said with a sigh.

Laurie joined the group at the counter. "I'm not sure we need to race, but teams sound like a good idea. If we can mix two batches of cook-

71

ies at once, the work will get done twice as fast."

"I'm working with Maria," Caroline said quickly.

Patricia said, "I wanted to be on Vicki's team anyway. So I don't care."

With the recipe in her hand, Laurie told everyone what to put in each batch of cookies. Then she went back to her math homework.

Caroline popped some sticks of butter into the microwave to soften. Maria measured the white sugar and the brown sugar before she dumped them into their big bowl.

"Mix this with the other stuff," Caroline told Maria as she poured melted butter into the bowl. "I'm going to mash the banana."

"Mmm . . . " Vicki said. "I *love* peanut butter-banana-marshmallow-surprise cookies."

Laurie said, "Tell me when it's time to put some cookies into the oven."

Caroline scraped the peanut butter out of the measuring cup and into the bowl. Next, Maria poured in the flour. Caroline stuck her big spoon into the batter and it stood up straight. This was the hardest part of making the cookies. It wasn't easy stirring the thick dough. She glanced across the counter in time to see Vicki yank an egg out of Patricia's hand. Then she bashed it on the side of the bowl. Egg goo and parts of shell dripped into the batter.

Vicki didn't seem very concerned. She stuck her hand right into the dough and picked out a piece of eggshell.

Caroline made a gagging noise. "Gross!"

"I'll fix it," Patricia muttered. She grabbed a spoon and carefully scooped the tiny pieces of eggshell out of the cookie batter while Caroline and Maria rolled their dough into little balls and set them on a flat pan. Then Laurie slid the pan into the oven and set the timer for eight minutes.

"We'll start mixing another batch right away," Maria said. "Don't worry, Caroline. We'll get it all done. Let's talk about tomorrow."

"Is your costume ready?" Caroline asked.

"Yeah. You're going to love it." Maria poured a cup of sugar into the mixing bowl. "Are you still coming over to my house in the morning?"

"Sure." Caroline measured a cup of sugar and dumped it into the bowl. "Your mom is

going to curl my hair—at least the hair that sticks out of my cap."

Maria used a spoon to pack the brown sugar into the measuring cup. "She invited your sisters, too. She wants to make sure they all look perfect." She stirred the brown sugar into the sugar that was already in the bowl. When she finished, she bent closer and peered at the mix. "This doesn't look right. Last time, the sugar looked more brown when I put the two kinds together." Maria shook her head. "I put one cup of white sugar in, and then I measured one cup of brown sugar . . . . "

Caroline said, "*You* put white sugar in the bowl?"

"Of course. It's my job."

Caroline groaned. "But *I* put in a cup of white sugar, too."

"Oh, no. It's wrecked!" Maria rested her elbows on the counter.

"No, it's not." Caroline took more softened butter out of the microwave. "We'll just put in two of everything—"

"And make a double batch!" Maria said, finishing Caroline's sentence for her.

The oven timer buzzed and Laurie pulled the

first cookie tray out of the oven. "They look delicious. Is there another batch ready?"

"Here's ours," Patricia said, carrying a bowl of lumpy dough to the oven. "But we need some help."

"I couldn't make the spoon move," Vicki explained.

Laurie mixed the dough. Then the little girls helped her roll it into balls.

"She'll want ours next," Maria said, cracking an egg on the side of the bowl.

Caroline handed her a second egg. "Yeah. And won't she be surprised when we give her a double batch?"

"Is it midnight yet?" Caroline asked the baby sitter several batches later.

Checking her watch, Laurie shook her head. "It's only nine-thirty."

Mrs. Santiago had picked Maria up around nine o'clock. Half an hour before that, Caroline's little sisters had gone into the family room and fallen asleep. Mr. and Mrs. Zucker hadn't come home yet, so Caroline and Laurie were on their own.

Laurie put down her math book and came

over to the counter. Since no one was using Vicki and Patricia's mixing bowl, she started measuring some sugar. Caroline had lost count of how many cookies they had made.

Finally Laurie pulled the last tray of cookies out of the oven. "This is it. We're done!"

"But Laurie . . . " Caroline piled one shoe box full of cookies on top of several others and frowned at the three batches of cookies still waiting to be packed. "There's nothing to put them into. I've run out of boxes."

Laurie opened several of the containers to count the cookies. When she finished, she asked, "How many batches were you supposed to bake?"

"Ten. Do we have enough?"

"Too many. There's at least fifteen batches here," Laurie said, to Caroline's dismay.

"I don't want Mom to know I messed up and made too many," Caroline whispered.

"Find something else to hold the rest of them," Laurie said. She squinted as if she was planning something really sneaky. "We'll just put all the containers into grocery bags and your mom won't know how many cookies are inside."

Caroline was impressed. She'd have to remember to ask Laurie for advice the next time she had a problem.

10

FISH HEADS AND TURKEY LEGS

"Do you *believe* Duncan?" Maria whispered during the fair the next day.

"What's he supposed to be? It looks like he's wearing a fish head." Caroline wrinkled her nose when he walked by thcm. Maybe it was crazy, but she thought she smelled tuna.

Duncan suddenly turned around and scowled at them. "What are you, Maria? A dumb bird?" he asked.

She grinned and stretched her arms. Her costume was awesome. When Maria held her arms straight, it was plain she was a flag.

Caroline didn't like being ignored, even by

Duncan. As promised, Mrs. Santiago had left a needle hanging from one of the stars, so she took it and pretended to sew the last star into place.

Duncan shook his head. "Cute, Maria. But I wouldn't let Zucker touch me if I were you."

Caroline bit her tongue to keep herself from punching him right in his fish face. Everyone knew Betsy Ross wouldn't have done anything like that.

Maria tugged on Caroline's sleeve. "Look over there. Doesn't Vicki look cute?"

Caroline's little sister was at the next game booth. She was trying to knock over some soda bottles by throwing a ball at them. But her first toss didn't even reach the bottles. When Vicki tried to lean over the front of the booth, her Little Pillow costume got in the way and she kind of bounced back a step.

Getting as close to the booth as her padded costume would allow, Vicki took the ball and threw it as hard as she could. It totally missed all three bottles.

Caroline patted her on the shoulder. "Nice try."

"But I didn't knock down any bottles," Vicki pouted.

"Would you like to try throwing a ball at something else?" Caroline asked with a grin.

Vicki looked around the gym. "Where?"

Caroline pointed to Duncan. "You see the guy with the fish head? Could you hit *him?*"

Maria stamped her foot. "Caroline Zucker! You can't get your baby sister in trouble like that!"

"I suppose you're right," she sighed. "Forget it, Vicki."

Maria changed the subject. "Have you bought any peanut butter-banana-marshmallow-surprise cookies?"

Caroline moaned. "I can't even stand to *look* at them after last night!"

"I couldn't face them either," Maria said. "But I've seen lots of people buying them."

Caroline grinned. "Good!"

Just then, Michael Hopkins walked past them in a turkey costume saying, "Gobble, gobble."

Caroline's eyes opened wide. "He's the bravest guy I know!" she said. She couldn't stop staring at Michael. His turkey costume with its big tail was very clever. But his legs! "What other guy would walk around in brown tights in *public?*"

Maria giggled as she said, "He does have good bird legs. I mean, they're real skinny."

"Hi, Patricia!" Vicki called loudly. When the girl in the golden crown didn't turn around, she pulled on Caroline's sleeve. "Patricia won't talk to me!"

"That isn't Patricia," Caroline explained. "She's too tall. And her hair's too long." She glanced around the gym. There were several princesses, and there were a few other girls wearing old-fashioned dresses like her Betsy Ross costume. But there was only one thirteen-star flag, one Little Pillow, and one boy in a turkey suit!

"Is everyone having fun?" Principal Fletcher asked from the low stage at the far end of the gym.

"Yes!" Caroline yelled along with hundreds of other kids.

"You all look wonderful," he told them. "And now it's time for the costume awards."

Maria reached for Caroline's hand and

squeezed it. "Do you think we'll win?" she asked.

Caroline tried to look confident as she replied, "Of course. No one else looks as neat as us."

"Right!" Maria agreed.

The two kindergarten teachers walked onto the stage and handed the principal a folded sheet of paper. He opened it and stepped closer to the microphone. "We'll start with the kindergarten classes. The winner is . . . Vicki Zucker."

Caroline clapped so hard that her hands hurt. As Vicki trotted up the steps and walked to the center of the stage, three of her feathers came unglued and fluttered to the floor. When Principal Fletcher handed her a huge stuffed bear, her arms were barely long enough to wrap around it, and she couldn't see over it. Her teacher had to help her find her way back down to the gym floor.

"First-grade teachers, I need your decision," the principal called into the microphone. He lifted a see-through case filled with bright markers. "This is the first-grade prize."

"It's going to be me," Patricia whispered into Caroline's ear.

Thinking about all the other princesses, Caroline said, "Maybe."

One of the first-grade teachers handed a note to the principal. He cleared his throat and bent close to his microphone. "The first-grade prize goes to . . . "

Next to Caroline, her sister whispered, "Patricia Zucker!"

But Principal Fletcher said, "Brian McDowell."

"Brian McDowell! That's disgusting!" Patricia's face turned red and she didn't look much like a princess anymore.

Caroline knew why Brian had won. His spider costume was very original—he'd been hitting people with his eight legs all day.

The second-grade prize went to a girl dressed up like a baby. She had pinned a big diaper over her pink ballet leotard and tights.

Then the third-grade teachers walked onto the stage. Caroline and Maria reached for each other's hands. Caroline wanted to win so much that she could barely breathe.

The principal held up an envelope. "I have

ten passes to Skate World here. The winner will be able to have a party for all of his or her friends."

"I *love* Skate World," Maria said. "If I win, you can come to my roller skating party."

It was then Caroline realized that only *one* of them could have the *best* costume. And she didn't think her Betsy Ross was the most amazing costume in the third grade.

Principal Fletcher read the teachers' note and laughed. "We have a tie! In this case, each winner will get five Skate World passes."

Maria put her mouth close to Caroline's ear. "It *has* to be us!"

Caroline happily agreed. "Who else could it be? I mean, it's a tie. And we're a pair."

"The Skate World passes go to . . . Michael Hopkins—and Duncan Fairbush."

Even though she was disappointed, Caroline clapped softly when Michael took his five passes from the principal. But when Duncan reached for his passes, she put her hands behind her back.

"What's he really supposed to be?" Maria asked. "I still haven't figured it out."

Caroline made a face. "I don't know the

name, but I think it's something from those dumb comic books he reads."

"He's Master Fishwich," a first-grade boy in front of them said. He seemed to think they were pretty stupid for not recognizing the famous fish monster.

"Master Fishwich?" Maria wrinkled her nose.

Caroline started to grin. "You know, Duncan *is* kinda slimy. I think his fish costume is perfect. In fact, maybe we should start calling him Fish Face Fairbush."

"Fish Face Fairbush." Maria repeated. Then she grinned. "I love it!"

"Caroline?" Mrs. Nicks was standing by their class booth as the fair ended. "We have some cookies left. Would you like to take them home?"

"How many are there?" Caroline asked.

Mrs. Nicks picked up two big boxes. "There must be four or five dozen in here. I don't understand it. I saw people eating these cookies all day long. We should have run out of them. How many cookies did you bake?"

"Too many," Caroline mumbled.

"That's no problem." Mrs. Nicks didn't seem to think too many cookies was a disaster. "You can just take the extra ones home."

"No, I can't." Caroline said. How could she bring home five dozen peanut butter-banana-marshmallow-surprises? Her mother would know she'd made too many and she'd probably think Caroline was still a silly little kid.

She looked her teacher right in the eye. "Please don't make me take the cookies home, Mrs. Nicks."

"What should I do with them then?"

"Maybe you could have them," Caroline suggested.

Mrs. Nicks shook her head. "There aren't enough people at my house to eat all these cookies." Then she smiled. "I have an idea! I can take them to the homeless shelter. Would you like that?"

Caroline grinned. It was a wonderful solution. "I'd like that a lot!"

"Ah, Caroline . . . " Mrs. Nicks wiggled her finger, motioning Caroline to come closer, then bent down and spoke softly so no one else could hear. "I just wanted to tell you I voted for you and Maria in the costume contest. It's our secret, but you may tell Maria."

Caroline felt like she might explode from happiness. She waved good-bye to her teacher and ran to find her sisters and Maria.

They were waiting for her on the school sidewalk. Caroline whipped off her Betsy Ross cap and rushed over to them. "You'll never believe what happened—"

"Do you like my bear?" Vicki said, interrupting her. "His name is Shaggy Bear."

"You sure were lucky today," Caroline told her youngest sister. She tried to hug her, but the pillow costume got in the way. Then she turned to Maria and whispered, "But Vicki's not the only lucky one. You won't believe what Mrs. Nicks told me! She liked our costumes best. She voted for us! And she's giving the extra cookies to the homeless shelter so my mom won't find out I made such a big mistake. And that's not all." Caroline grinned. "I'm going to surprise everyone on Monday when I wear another new outfit. Maybe I'll wear the dress!"

Maria giggled. "Do you think everyone is ready for it?"

"For my new clothes?"

Maria nodded. "Yes. Are they ready for the New-and-Improved Caroline Zucker?"

"I hope *one* person isn't ready," she told Maria. "I hope Fish Face Fairbush *chokes* when he sees me!"